I0537775

Four Phoenixes Press
© 2017Jennifer L. Gadd
ISBN-13: 978-0692980606
ISBN-10: 0692980601

SPACE BUGS

Jennifer L. Gadd

"It's not our differences that divide us. It is our inability to recognize, accept, and celebrate those differences."

–Audra Lorde

Chapter 1: Escape!

Zach Bergman strapped on the life suit and zipped himself in. What had he been thinking? He had been looking forward to a totally boring month at space camp. Well, not exactly looking forward. This was the same space camp he and his friends had been coming to every summer since forever. He was fifteen now, for crying out loud, and camp was for babies. It was always the same: sissy hikes down the moon crater, making stupid keychains out of pseudo-leather, nasty mystery meat meals from the syntho-cooker. He had seen it all and done it all. Or so he'd thought.

Now here he was, watching smoke curl up through what was left of the bay door seal. He glanced nervously over his shoulder. The hot smell of burning plastic and wire hit his nostrils. As soon as the wires burned through, the door would slide open. And chances were the Gregarians would be on the other side, ready to swarm back in.

He glanced across the launching pad as Trudy Jackson helped another boy get his huge feet into his suit the right way. What a dork! Zach checked the breathing vent on his suit to make sure it was working right. One week. They had been at camp one week and all hell was breaking loose.

Zach turned back to the other two teenagers and said, "Time's up. We gotta move out now!" Trudy grabbed her helmet and headed towards the lifepod. It was their only way out of the campground. Brian Walsh was still struggling into his suit. Zach picked up Brian's helmet and slammed it into his chest, hard. "Now, loser," he repeated.

Hurrying, Brian tripped over his own feet and stumbled. Zach grabbed him by the front of his survival suit and pushed him roughly towards the lifepod. With a sneer, Zach taunted, "You know what I'll do to you if you don't get that helmet on before we take off?" Brian turned pale and shook his head. Zach laughed and said, "Nothing. You'll be dead already!"

"Shut up, jerk." Trudy stuck her head back through the sliding door of the lifepod and frowned at the two boys. Her brown face was slick with sweat.

"Well, it's the truth," Zach pointed out as he climbed into the pod. He plopped in front of the controls and flipped on the power.

Hundreds of colored lights blinked on. Dials glowed in the dim light.

Soft beeps and hums told them the machine was running.

Trudy eyed the two boys. "So," she said, "anybody know how to drive this thing?"

Zach poked at a button, and Trudy's hand shot out to stop him. He slumped back into the chair and shook his head. A voice from the doorway spoke up quietly. "Uh, guys? My uncle used to let me drive his cargo mover once in a while. You know, for practice."

Trudy and Zach turned and gaped at Brian. Trudy spoke up first. "You can drive?"

Brian shrugged. "A little," he answered, "I mean I have before."

"No way," said Zach, but his words were drowned out by the loud, scraping sound of the bay door opening. Smoke billowed into the docking bay, and they knew the Gregarians would attack at any moment.

"Yes, way," said Trudy. She poked him in the chest, making him wince. This was no time to argue, so he threw himself into a rear seat. Trudy pointed at Brian and said, "Let's go, flyboy." Brian turned bright red and sat down in front of the controls.

He wiped his sweaty palms on his thighs. His pushed his dark hair out of eyes and pored over the panel of lights and buttons, searching for something that looked familiar. Leave it to the camp to have a pod so old the labels were worn right off all the controls! He cleared his throat nervously, one hand hovering over what he hoped was the ignition.

He was just about to press the button when a loud crash distracted him. The bay door was hanging on its hinges, and the tall, brown Gregarians stormed through the door with a buzz of wings.

"Now, Brian!" shouted Trudy. "They've gotten through!"

Brian pushed the green button to his left and gave a sigh of relief as machine rose and hovered over the cargo bay.

"Buckle up," said Brian.

"Just go, man. Don't be a wuss," came from the back seat.

"I'm not leaving until you buckle up," Brian replied. The tall Gregarian fired his weapon, and what looked like a green tractor beam hit the wall above the lifepod.

"Just do it, stupid! They're trying to catch us with a tractor beam!" Trudy commanded, as she fastened her own harness. Lasers heated up the wall of the bay near their pod.

Brian eased the steering wand forward with shaking hands. Sweat beaded up on his forehead. The lifepod jolted forward and wobbled left and right. He aimed for the bay door and pushed the wand hard. The lifepod shot forward and bounced off the side of the bay before hurtling into the air.

"Nice going, loser!" Zach muttered.

"Would you just shut up?" said Trudy. "I'd be nervous, too, if someone yelled at me all the time!"

Zach fell into an angry silence, and Brian took a deep breath. The hard part was over, and they had escaped.

Suddenly, there was a loud boom, and the wand jerked out of Brian's hand. The lifepod rolled over and whatever the Gregarians had blown up hurtled them out toward space!

"Do something!" screamed Trudy. "If we leave orbit, we can't get back!

This thing isn't designed for out of orbit flight!"

"I know that!" said Brian frantically. He just wasn't sure what he could do about it. He pulled back on the steering wand and tried to stop the pod's spinning. Finally, they quit rolling and just rocked back and forth in jerky motions. Eventually, Brian was able to steady the small craft into an even flight.

Trudy looked out the console window at the bleak lunar landscape. "So," she said blankly, "where are we?"

Zach leaned forward to look. He pointed off into the distance to a plume of smoke that rose into the sky. "There, that's what's left of the campground," he said. "Stupid grasshoppers."

"The Gregarians aren't grasshoppers, you idiot," Trudy exclaimed.

They argued back and forth until Brian spoke up. "Yeah, they are."

The other two stopped. "What?" Trudy and Zach said.

"They are. Insectoid, I mean. Genetically. They're big, super-intelligent grasshoppers."

Trudy shuddered. "So now what?" she asked. Her voice began to crack, and she knew she sounded afraid.

Zach rummaged around in the wall compartments in the backseat. "We're in luck!" he said. "There's some E-rations back here." He tore open a box of the standard issue emergency food packs and tossed nutrition bars over the front seats.

"We'd better save them until we're really hungry," Trudy pointed out. "I mean, this might be all the food left on the whole moon."

"There's a cave over there," Zach said. He pointed towards a line of ridged mountains in the near distance.

"How do you know that?" Trudy asked.

Zach gave her a look and shrugged. "That's where my friends and I go party all the time," he said.

Trudy rolled her eyes in disgust. "You're hopeless, dude," she said.

Brian turned the lifepod towards the mountain ridge and started to land.

Chapter 2: Assessing the Damage

Brian rolled over in his sleeping bag and stared up at the ceiling of the cave. The rock, he thought, must have quartz in it because it sparkled in the light of the lightbox they'd found in the lifepod. He couldn't sleep.

"You awake?" Trudy whispered.

"Yeah," he said.

"Me, too," came from Zach's sleeping bag.

"Guys," said Trudy, "what are we gonna do?"

No one had an answer, so the cave got quiet. The moon had just enough atmosphere and oxygen, mostly due to the aqua-synth machines that made water for the camp, so that after nightfall, they could breathe easily without lifesuits as long as they weren't too active. But no action made them sitting ducks for the Gregarians.

Finally Trudy's small voice expressed her fear. "We're going to run out of oxygen, aren't we? We're going to die."

"Shut up!" yelled Zach. He jumped up and charged across the cave at her. "Just shut up, okay?" That small exertion, however, almost took his breath away. He stood there gasping, and Trudy's fear suddenly became a very real possibility.

"Lie down and be still, stupid," muttered Brian. "You're sucking all the air out of the place."

Zach started to get even, but he realized Brian was right. Plus, he didn't have enough breath to punch him. He lay back down on his sleeping bag and tried to breathe.

"Don't call me stupid, stupid," he retorted.

Trudy sighed. "Guys," she said, "we're it, remember? We're the only ones we've got to get ourselves out of this. Can you both just get over yourselves?"

The boys looked embarrassed, but stopped bickering. "So," Trudy said, "we have shelter, at least for now. Beyond that?"

"Air," said Zach. "We need air, and we don't know for how long."

"So how do we get new life suits?" Trudy asked. "They were stored in the space dock."

"We could try to sneak in," said Zach.

Trudy rolled her eyes. "Zach, try not to be completely stupid, okay. The Gregarians blew up the space dock!"

Zach rolled over. "Oh yeah," he said, "I forgot."

"You forgot," muttered Trudy. The three teenagers got quiet.

After a long while, Brian said, "Guys? I have an idea."

"Let's hear it, brainiac," said Zach.

The other two could almost hear Brian's brain whirring in the near darkness. "The camp's aqua-synth machines are in a storehouse near the gardens, right?"

"Right," answered Trudy.

"And that's on the other end of camp from the space dock."

"Yeah," said Zach.

"I think I can convert one to make air instead of water," he explained. "All I'd have to do is program it to make nitrogen instead of hydrogen. A few more electrons per atom is all."

"Nitrogen?" asked Trudy. "Why nitrogen?"

"Nitrogen makes up most of the earth's atmosphere. I'll program the synth machine to make nitrogen and oxygen, instead of hydrogen and oxygen, which make water. We can make enough breathable air to refill the tanks on the lifesuits."

"You can do that?" Trudy asked.

"I'm pretty sure, yeah," Brian said. "It shouldn't be too hard."

Zach finally spoke. "So all we need to do is sneak past the grasshoppers and steal a machine. Any idea how we do that?"

No one spoke. No one had any ideas.

"Guys," said Trudy. "We have enough oxygen for now. We need to get some sleep so we can think better. I'm too tired to think. We'll have to scope out the situation eventually, but let's save it for morning."

The next morning, they were up before the bright blue sun rose in the horizon, before it started heating the small moon's thin atmosphere and they couldn't breathe. They put on their life-suits and fired up the space pod.

"Hey," said Zach, "how about we fly around the front of the camp first to see what's going on? There's that line of hills almost all the way around the perimeter of the camp."

Trudy snickered. "You really do know all the ways to sneak around places, don't you?" Zach shrugged and grinned, as Trudy continued, "I don't know. Maybe we should do this as quickly as possible."

Brian considered before steering the pod. "Zach has a good idea. We need to know what the Gregarians are up to. Otherwise, we won't know where to hide because we won't know where they are." He guided the pod around the other way.

His hand paused over the lift button. "I think we should stay low. I'm putting it on hover."

They flew low to the ground until they came around to the camp entrance. They pulled up behind the low ridge of hills that went three-fourths of the way around the camp. Brian idled the engine.

"Why are you stopping?" Trudy asked. Brian gestured to the camp office building, about a hundred yards away.

Trudy's mouth fell open.

"What the heck are they doing?" Zach exploded.

The Gregarians were swarming all over the front yard of the office building. Most surprising, though, were the holes pitting the moon's surface. The Gregarians were digging everything up!

They could hear the faint humming sound the Gregarians used to communicate. They couldn't understand it, but even from this far, they could hear that it sounded urgent.

"They're looking for something!" Trudy realized. She got very quiet as she thought about it. "I think we need to find out what they're looking for. I think it's important."

"Sure," said Zach. "I'll sign up for Gregarian classes just as soon as we get out of here."

Trudy didn't answer. But she had an idea. "Let's go get that synth machine," was all she said.

Brian moved the space pod along the far side of the hills. "We have to be careful. It won't take much for them to see us."

"So what exactly do grasshoppers see?" wondered Trudy.

Brian paused. "Everything," he said. "They can't see as much detail as we can, but they're way, way better at seeing motion. They'll see us move even if we think we're standing perfectly still. Let's get out of here."

Brian maneuvered the space pod all the way around to the back of campground. This was where all the gardens that provided food were laid out. It was also where the hills ended. They would be exposed.

He stepped on the gas and moved between the trees in the orchard to stay hidden. It didn't make any sense because the Gregarians would see the movement before they'd see the pod, but he couldn't help it.

Across the field, right in front of them, was the storage building. Brian drove straight in and cut the engine so it wouldn't vibrate. He whispered to the other two, "No talking! They'll feel it."

He jumped out and ran over to where a long row of synth machines were stored. Many of them were too large for him even to lift, but he found one that was small enough to carry, but large enough to make enough air for them. As he returned to the pod, he saw Trudy store a small machine in the back of the pod.

He looked at with a puzzled look, but didn't speak.

"Ask me later." she said, "Let's just get out of here!" Then her eyes got big. She had forgotten not to talk! Brian rolled his eyes at the sound of her voice.

Zach, who had been watching at the door and he turned around in a panic. "They heard you! Or felt you! Or whatever! They're coming!"

The three of them jumped into the space pod, and Brian gunned the engine and shot out of the storage shed.

He headed out across the bleak moon landscape, not knowing where he was going. The Gregarians were hot on their trail.

Chapter Three: Exploration

"They're right behind us!" screamed Trudy.

"Get us out of here!" yelled Zach.

"I'm trying, I'm trying!" hollered Brian.

The Gregarians were almost on top of them.

"We can't outrun them," Brian shouted over their screams. "There's only one thing I can think of—"

Brian pushed a button on the dashboard, and suddenly all the windows went dark.

Trudy screamed again. "I can't see!"

Brian ignored her and cut the engine. The life pod dropped to the ground and sat where it was, motionless. There they were, right in the middle of an open field, waiting for the Gregarians to get them.

"What do you think you're doing, stupid?" Zach pulled back his hand as if he intended to hit Brian.

Brian, instead of cowering, turned on Zach. "Shut up!" he said. "I'm sick of your bullying, and I'm sick of being treated like crap. Sit down and shut up." The buzzing of insect wings was nearing, and Zach, shocked, sat down and shut up.

"What have you done, Brian?" Trudy asked as the buzzing got even louder.

"What I think I've done is save our butts," Brian answered. "They can only see movement, remember? Well, we're not moving. And they can't see us move around in here with the windows dark. Now both of you just be quiet so they don't pick up the vibrations from our vocal chords."

It got very quiet inside the lifepod. Outside the humming was right on top of them. The Gregarians flew right over them as if they weren't even there. After a long while, it was as quiet outside as it was inside.

It stayed quiet for a long time. Brian hesitated and then said, "Nobody move." He pushed the button again, and the windows became transparent. The Gregarians were nowhere to be seen. Carefully, Brian steered the lifepod back to their cave.

Still shaken, they climbed out of the pod. Zach looked uncomfortable and said, "Hey, about what I said." He looked embarrassed. "Sorry I gave you a hard time. I guess . . . I guess I was just scared or something."

Brian rolled his eyes. "Or something. Yeah, right," he said.

"You know, you really need to stop being such an a—"

"Stop it, you two. Both of you just get over yourselves," Trudy cut in. "You," she gestured towards Brian, "we need some air, and you said you could do it."

Brian nodded and pulled the equipment out of the lifepod. "It'll take a couple of hours, I'm guessing," he said.

"In the meantime," Trudy added, "Zach and I are going to explore this cave." To her surprise, he agreed.

"Geology is, like, my thing," he said. They left Brian in the front of the cave with the hydro-machine and a communicator. "Anything happens, call us," Trudy said.

Brian grinned, "If anything happens, I'm running into the cave with you guys." Trudy grinned back.

Zach grabbed a torch, and he and Trudy set out. The cave looked solid and as far as they could see, the ceiling was high enough for them to stand up. Zach shone the light up the walls. The quartz glittered in the light.

"Igneous rock," Zach pointed out.

"So?" Trudy asked.

"It's volcanic, that's what. This moon has active volcanoes, you know. The camp uses them for geothermal power."

Trudy looked worried. "No, I didn't know that," she said. They walked down the length of the cave for about a half hour, when Trudy noticed something. "Hey, we're doing downhill, aren't we?"

"Yeah," said Zach. "The cave is sloping down, so we're farther underground than we were a few minutes ago. It's getting pretty steep, too."

They came to a place where the cave split off into two pathways.

Trudy shone the light down the path on the right. From where they were, they could see that path started sloping back up to the surface of the moon. One look at the path on the left told them it went deeper towards the moon's center. They looked at each other with scared looks, but they knew which way they had to go.

They hadn't gone more than ten paces, when suddenly the ground began to tremble. It was ever so slight, but they could feel the tremor.

Zach stopped and pulled out a small machine about the size of a deck of cards. He fiddled with the controls and said, "Well that's just great."

Trudy looked at him with real fear in her eyes. "I take it that was not a good thing," she said.

"You could say that, yeah. This is a seismograph. We've got some activity down there."

"What?" exclaimed Trudy. "A volcano is going to erupt?"

Zach took a deep breath. "Maybe."

"Maybe! Zach, the correct answer was no!" Trudy pleaded.

"Sorry," he said. "No guarantees, of course, but it's a possibility. Let's keep going."

Before long, the cave widened into a large chamber. Trudy shone the light inside, and they both gasped. The entire surface of the floor of the chamber was full of holes. At the far end, the wall of the chamber was caved in, making a pile of rocks.

"What in the world—" said Trudy. Before she could finish her question, the sound of someone running up from behind frightened her. She dropped the light she was holding, and suddenly everything went pitch dark and whatever was running grabbed her and started screaming!

Chapter 4: Discovery

Almost as soon as whatever it was grabbed her, Trudy felt it let go. She could hear screaming and punches being thrown. She heard grunts and gasps and—

"Brian?" she asked. "Is that you?"

"Get him off of me!" Brian yelled. "Zach, you idiot!"

"I'm an idiot," Zach yelled back. "*I'm* an idiot! Who's the one sneaking up on people and screaming like a little girl?"

"Hey," said Trudy, "that's not funny."

Trudy had been feeling around in the sandy floor of the cave and found the light. She switched it on. Zach had pushed Brian to the floor and was sitting on top of him. Brian was struggling hard to push Zach off. Both were in a panic and neither could see what he was doing, so they were mostly just swatting at the air.

Trudy started to laugh. The boys looked over at her, on her knees in the dirt, and then at each other with their arms flailing around the air. They started to laugh, too. Trudy said, "Okay, maybe it's a little bit funny."

Once they had calmed down, Zach said, "What in the world were you doing, man?"

"Well, I had just finished converting the hydro-synth—and it works, by the way, thank me very much—when the tremor started. I ran down here to see if you guys were okay. Next thing I knew, it went all dark and somebody jumped me. You!"

Trudy giggled again. The boys grinned at each other. All three of them stood up and slapped the dust off their lifesuits. They began to explore the cave chamber.

Trudy and Zach pointed the light towards the caved-in wall. Brian, though, became very interested in one of the holes in the floor of the chamber. He dropped down on his knees and began digging in the dirt around one of the holes.

At the exact same time, Zach and Brian both said, "Uh, guys, I think you need to come to look at this!" Brian looked up in time to see Trudy backing away from the pile of rocks looking as if she might throw up.

"What is it?" Brian asked.

"I don't know," said Trudy. "Worms or something. That's the grossest thing I've ever seen in my life!"

"There are more?" Brian asked.

"More? What you do mean, more?" she said.

He pointed down into the hole. Inside were about fifteen white pods, about two feet long. They looked like huge grains of rice.

Trudy looked as if she might faint. "What are they, Brian?" she asked. But before he could answer, there was another tremor, and everything began to shake. Brian and Trudy fell to the ground, as Zach stumbled over to them. He dropped to the ground beside them.

The tremor stopped after a few seconds. "So," said Zach. "What's going on here?"

"Yeah, what are those horrible things?" Trudy asked again.

"Egg sacs," said Brian. "Larvae."

"Eggs?" Trudy asked. She looked confused.

"I think we've found what the Gregarians are looking for, is what. These are insect eggs."

Zach whistled through his teeth. "So this whole place is nothing but a freaking baby nursery," he said.

"Right," said Brian. "Gregarians lay eggs like other grasshoppers, and their young are hatched in a near-adult form—not like, say, caterpillars that turn into butterflies. They're called nymphs."

Trudy looked thoughtful. "So," she said, "they've come back for their children."

"It looks like it," said Brian. "Gregarians lay their eggs in nests like these. They take a long time and the right conditions to hatch, but they do return to care for them. They have that in common with humans—they take care of their kids."

"And what are the right conditions?" Zach asked. He was pretty sure he didn't want to hear the answer.

"It has to be warm enough for them to hatch," Brian said.

"And would you say that something like, oh, volcanic activity that brings magma close to the surface of the moon would make it warm enough?"

Trudy groaned. Brian sat back on his heels and looked at Zach seriously. "Yeah," he answered, "that would pretty much be warm enough."

Another short rumble told them they needed to get back up to the surface of the moon. Zach and Trudy protested, but Brian insisted on carrying one of the egg sacs back up to the cave.

"It's sleeping with you, though!" Trudy said.

They settled down for the night after taking off their life-suits and turning the light-box over to "heat."

The night was getting chilly. Soon their cave was toasty warm.

They were sound asleep when a red light started flashing on and off in their faces. At first, they were not awake enough to figure out what was going on, but soon Trudy said, "It's the communicator. I picked it up in the storage shed."

She grabbed the small box and punched some buttons. The red light did not stop blinking. Trudy set the box down.

"They're coming to get us," she said.

"Who is?" asked Brian.

"I don't know exactly, but they know about the Gregarians, and they're coming."

"That's good, I guess."

"Yeah," she said, "except I didn't send them a message. I can't communicate out on this thing. They only know about the Gregarians. They don't know about us."

"What does that mean?"

"It means that they think all the humans are dead—"

"And they'll just come blow everything up—"

"Including us."

Just then Zach made a noise that sounded like he was choking. They turned around just in time to see the little grasshopper nymph climb out of what was left of the egg sac and take a small hop towards them.

Chapter 5: Rescue!

No one moved. No one except the little grasshopper. It stood about the height of a toddler, and its head tilted from side to side as if it was trying to figure them out. It took another little hop towards Zach. He moved back, and it hopped closer.

Zach froze, terrified. One antenna reached out slowly and touched his face. Then the creature hopped towards him again. It didn't seem to be attacking, so Zach relaxed.

They all sat down again around the heater and exhaled loudly. They were about to be rescued, but they didn't feel very safe!

The little grasshopper gave a little hop and joined their circle, sitting by Zach's feet.

"What are we going to do with this—this—this thing?" he asked.

"She," said Brian.

"What?" said the other two.

"The nymph is a girl. You can tell by the shape of the abdomen."

"A girl. Great," said Zach. "I'll be sure to get a pink bonnet next time at the store."

The insect had settled down by Zach and seemed to have fallen asleep. She was making a soft little chirp as she slept. Zach frowned.

"So what does it—I mean she— eat?" asked Trudy.

"Anything," said Brian. "They'll eat any kind of plant that grows."

They sat up for a while, watching the sleeping grasshopper as if afraid she might still wake up and attack them. They tried to come up with a way to let the rescue team know they were still on the moon. They finally decided to go to sleep and wait for morning.

When Trudy and Brian woke up in the morning, Zach and the grasshopper weren't in the cave. The chirping sound, however, led them outside.

Zach grinned, embarrassed. "She follows me everywhere," he said.

Brian laughed. "Maybe she thinks you're her mother!" he joked.

"That's totally not funny!" Zach said.

The grasshopper was munching her way through a patch of grass near the cave. Trudy watched her closely.

"We need to take her back," she said.

The boys nodded. "Maybe," Brian said, "the Gregarians won't kill us if we have her with us."

"Or maybe they'll think we captured her," Trudy said.

"It's still the only thing we can do. We can't keep her fed properly out here. There's not enough grass or trees," Zach said. "C'mon, Hopper. We have to go."

As if she understood him, the nymph followed Zach over to the space pod. Trudy and Brian looked at each other and smiled. "Hopper?" Brian asked.

Well," said Zach, "I had to call her something, didn't I?"

They got Hopper into the back of the pod, but she would only sit still if Zach sat next to her. Trudy climbed in beside Brian, and they took off back to the camp.

As they got near to the main camp, they could see three ships had landed not far away. The rescue squad had arrived!

Zach lifted Hopper out of the space pod, and she hopped over to a big clump of grass in the field. Men in red life-suits appeared almost instantly and raised their guns. Zach saw it, and he ran over to the little nymph and blocked their way. "No!" he yelled, "Don't shoot her!"

At the same time, they heard an angry humming noise coming near. The Gregarians had seen the rescue ships and were getting ready for a fight!

The men in the lifesuits stopped, not sure what to do. They did not want to hit Zach.

"Listen!" Zach yelled at the Gregarians. "We found your nest! The eggs are okay! Listen to me!"

The Gregarians could not understand what he was saying. They raised their guns at him.

With a loud chirp, Hopper jumped into his arms to block the path. Now the Gregarians did not know what to do.

Trudy spoke up. "They can't understand each other. Here, take the communicator I picked up. I thought it might come in handy."

She walked slowly with the small box to where Zach and Hopper were standing. No one would shoot while they were close together.

"You just talk into the speaker. I've set it for Gregarian already," she said.

Zach spoke into the microphone in English, and Gregarian came out of the speaker! He told them they had found had the egg nest and that the eggs were okay. He also told them about the volcano that was about to erupt. Their eggs were in danger! The Gregarians started humming again. This time they sounded worried.

All of a sudden, one of the rescue team came running over to them. "Zach!" the man called out.

"Dad?" said Zach. "Dad! Is that you?" He set Hopper down and hugged the man.

"What's going on here, son?"

A Gregarian hopped over to where Hopper was having another snack and spoke to Zach. Zach didn't know what he was saying, but he didn't sound angry. Hopper started jumping back and forth between them excitedly.

Another Gregarian hopped over with a communicator.

"This boy has taken care of our nymph. We thank him for this. It was not our intention to cause harm here. We did not understand that there was intelligent life on this moon. We only wanted to find our nest, which was laid here years ago for safety."

Zach's dad said, "This is a camp for our children, and you have destroyed them!"

The Gregarian shook his head. "No. We saw at once that the humans here were young and would need care. We tried to recover these three, but they ran away from us in their fear. Your nymphs are quite safe, as are their keepers. No one was harmed."

Zach's dad gave a sigh of relief and motion to the other men to go find the children.

Then Zach spoke up. "Dad," he said, "we need to help them save their eggs and any nymphs that have hatched. That volcano will kill them all."

Zach's dad looked at him for a moment. "Two weeks of summer camp has been good for you, Zach."

Zach grinned. "Yeah, I guess so. Anyway, I made some new friends." He pointed to Brian and Trudy, who grinned back at him. "Maybe I'm growing up."

Once they checked on the campers and made sure they were okay, the humans helped the Gregarians move the eggs and nymphs to their space ship. The adult humans and Gregarians began talking about business agreements between their two planets, and the children and nymphs played a kind of leapfrog game in the field.

Zach, Trudy, and Brian watched them play. They couldn't believe how everything had turned out. They had thought they would be killed, but they were safe. Instead of war between the Gregarians and the humans, there was peace.

"You know," Trudy said, "the little space bugs are kind of cute. They're growing on me." Brian and Zach laughed.

The Gregarians stayed for a few days to make repairs to the space dock they had damaged. Then it was time for them to go home. Just before they took off, Hopper came over to Zach to say good-bye. She had a communicator box with her.

"You are my friend," she said. "I will never forget you."

Zach cleared his throat hard. "Um, yeah. Don't be stranger, okay?"

Hopper looked confused. "I do not understand," she said.

"I mean I hope I see you again someday. Because we're friends."

Zach couldn't be sure, but it almost looked as if Hopper smiled. She lowered one feeler and touched him on the cheek. Then she hopped into the space ship and the door closed. The three friends waved good-bye as the Gregarian space ship took off.

As they watched the ship disappear, Zach said, "Well, another boring year at camp is over. Nothing exciting EVER happens around here."

Trudy laughed. Brian punched Zach in the arm and told him to shut up. Then the three friends walked back to the campgrounds together.

About the Author

Jennifer L. Gadd is a life-long reader and writer who holds a deep interest in writing books children and young adults want to read. She writes mostly fantasy and science fiction, as well as hi-lo books for struggling readers. She has lived in Texas, Illinois, and Alaska, and currently resides in Kansas City, Kansas, where she is a reading interventionist at an urban middle school. She lives in KCK with her husband and her Chihuahua, her two children being all grown up now. When she isn't writing or reading, you might find her baking, crocheting, hanging out in coffee shops, or rearranging the furniture.

You can find her lots of places on the Internet.

http://jennifergadd.wix.com/jenniferlgadd
https://www.facebook.com/jlgadd
https://jenniferlgadd.wordpress.com/
https://twitter.com/fionnabhar

www.ingramcontent.com/pod-product-compliance
Lightning Source LLC
Chambersburg PA
CBHW071215130626
46555CB00004B/1719